It's Freezing Out!

Written by Becca Heddle

Illustrated by Arief Putra

Collins

It's freezing! We pop on coats and boots. Then we step into the forest.

It is bright, and the air is crisp and clear. My scarf keeps my throat snug.

The rain turns to sleet, but my thick coat keeps out the damp.

Damp green weeds float on the pond.
Mist sweeps across it.

mist

weeds

Three brown rabbits creep out of the woods. They stop by a tree stump to sniff the air.

Our feet crunch in the frost. Look at the trail of footprints!

When it starts to get dark, we hear an owl screech.

owl

A stoat bursts out of the trees.
Is the owl hunting it?

stoat

9

Mum points out a star in the gloom.
It is bright.

star

Some flowers still bloom in the winter. They look like stars in the moonlight.

Soon my fingers start freezing.
We scoot back into our snug house.

I look out at the stars. I love winter, the clear nights and the frost.

We hear ...

We see ...

14

We feel ...

15

After reading

Letters and Sounds: Phase 4

Word count: 170

Focus on adjacent consonants with long vowel phonemes, e.g. *starts*.

Common exception words: of, to, the, I, into, by, my, we, they, like, some, when, out, house, love, our, there

Curriculum links: Science: Seasonal changes

National Curriculum learning objectives: Reading/word reading: apply phonic knowledge and skills as the route to decode words; read accurately by blending sounds in unfamiliar words containing GPCs that have been taught; read common exception words, noting unusual correspondences between spelling and sound and where these occur in the word; Reading/comprehension: being encouraged to link what they read or hear read to their own experiences; understand both the books they can already read accurately and fluently and those they listen to by making inferences on the basis of what is being said and done and vocabulary provided by the teacher

Developing fluency

- Take turns to read a page, ensuring your child pauses for full stops and commas and checking your child does not miss the labels.

Phonic practice

- Support your child in sounding out and blending the consonants and long vowel sounds. (e.g. t/r/ee)

- Ask your child to read these aloud:

  c/r/ee/p   s/w/ee/p/s   g/r/ee/n

  b/l/oo/m   g/l/oo/m   s/c/oo/t

  b/r/ow/n   s/t/ar/t/s   f/l/ow/er/s

Extending vocabulary

- Ask your child to find the word that is not a synonym for each of the following. (Support your child in reading the words if necessary.)

  snug: cool cosy warm (*cool*)

  damp: moist smelly dank (*smelly*)

  gloom: ice darkness half-light (*ice*)

  scoot: drive whizz nip (*drive*)